The Adventures of
The Swamp Kids

TuTu's Christmas on the Bayou

Written by *Leif Pedersen 2014*
Leif Nedland Pedersen

Layout and Illustrations by
Tim Banfell

Ally-Gator BookBites Publishing House

Published by
Ally-Gator BookBites Publishing House
1428 Watkins Street
Lake Charles, LA 70601
www.ally-gatorbookbites.com

Printed in the U.S.A. through Bolton Associates, Inc.
San Rafael, CA 94901
www.boltonprinting.com

First Printing
ISBN# 978-0-9886332-3-0

Our books are yummy!

Look for other titles and merchandise at
www.theswampkids.com

This Christmas book is dedicated to my father:

Einar N. Pedersen, Sr.

He was my hero in so many ways; a wonderful family man, devoted husband, student body leader, outstanding athlete, imaginative director of youth camping, self-taught musician, world-class composer & arranger of Barbershop music, lover of a good joke and a man who was admired by more people than anyone could ever imagine. It was Mr. Pete, Dad to us, who brought home the "needle-free" Christmas tree one holiday season when my sisters, brothers and I were very young and living in campus housing at Tulane University - the other love of his life. It is a story that has delighted family and friends for years and it continues to live on as the inspiration for this adventure of the Swamp Kids...

Leif Nedland Pedersen

Picture circa 1948: (left to right) Einar Jr., Ellen, Dad and Leif.
Yet to make an appearance, Ingrid, Kristian, Sr. and Karin

As TuTu looked out at the Bayou one winter
he thought, "What will this Christmas bring?
I hope lots of presents, hot chocolate and cookies
and plenty of carols to sing."

"But one thing is missing," he thought to himself

"it's a thing that we never do see;

the fact that we live hidden deep in this Bayou;

we've never had one Christmas tree."

"We light up our cypress trees, that's our tradition,

and everyone joins in the show;

and when we are finished and done with our magic,

the Bayou takes on a warm glow."

"But only just once I would like to have Christmas

the way that it's meant to be seen;

with ornaments, lights and some shiny bright tinsel

spread over a tall evergreen."

He walked from the bayou all filled with excitement

just thinking what pleasure he'd bring;

his joy turned to laughter and soon he was dancing

and with that he started to sing.

"A diddle ay iddle ayeeeeee!!!

A diddle ay iddle ayeeeeee!!!

I can't wait to see what will be our first tree,

a diddle ay iddle ayeeeeee!!!"

He skipped to a Christmas tree lot in the town

and he searched through it most of the day;

"I want this to be a real special surprise

and share joy the traditional way."

He suddenly saw a spectacular tree,

it stood seven feet tall end to end;

"It looks like I'll have to take hold with some rope

and then drag it back home to my friends."

The trip wasn't easy and what made it worse

was the rain now had started to pour.

He lowered his head as he thought of Pierre,

"If he knew he would help, that's for sure."

He finally reached home and he called to his friends,

"Come quick! I've got something to see!"

He smiled and he beamed as they came one by one,

he had brought them their first Christmas tree.

They stood and they stared and there wasn't a sound,

it was if things had come to an end;

some looked to the sky; others looked at the ground,

but not one of them looked at their friend.

When TuTu turned back and he saw what they saw,

there was nothing at all he could say.

The tree had no needles; not even a one

from the dragging it took on that day.

He hung down his head as he held back a tear

but Mon Cher would soon help save the day;

"My goodness," she said, "what a wonderful tree,"

and her smile washed his sadness away.

The Swamp Kids all danced as they circled the tree

and then grabbed him to join them in song;

they laughed as they sang and they sang through the night

and they danced as if nothing was wrong;

A diddle ay iddle ayeeeeee,
a diddle ay iddle ayeeeeee;

Our TuTu brought glee with
our own Christmas tree,

A diddle ay iddle ayeeeeee!!!

"Let's pass a good time!" said his good friend Pierre,

"this is something that no one should miss.

Put the presents and packages under the tree,

then I'll pin on our Santa Claus list."

They put on some ribbons and cones of bright colors;

the fireflies gave it their light;

Then TuTu said, "Let's all sing, Joyeux Noël!"

and they all had a very good night!

Our story line's simple and easy to see;

it is something you'll all want to learn;

"Whenever you give those you love something special,

you'll always feel good in return!"

Lagniappe Lesson

By Santa Claus

CHRISTMAS AROUND THE WORLD

Boys and Girls, here's a language trip you can take around the world with Mom, Dad or friends. We all know the words, Merry Christmas, because it's in the English language; some may also know it when they see it written in French, Joyeaux Noël, and still others may know it in Spanish, Feliz Navidad. But you may be surprised to see how it's written in other parts of the world.

Here are just a few examples - see how you do:

Afrikaans - **Gesëende Kersfees**

Brazil - **Christmas Alegre**

Bulgaria - **Весела Коледа**

Chinese - **Sheng Dan Kuai Le**

Czech - **Veselé Vánoce**

Dutch - **Vrolijk kerstfeest**

Greek - **Καλά Χριστούγεννα**

Hawaiian - **Mele Kalikimaka**

Hebrew - **Khag Same'ach**

Italy - **Buon Natale**

Japan - **Kurisumasu Omedeto**

Norwegian - **God Jul**

Polish - **Wesołych Świąt**

Russian - **С Рождеством**

Thai - **Suksun Wan Christmas**

Turkey - **Mutlu Noelle**

The words may look different when written, but in spirit, they all have the same message, "Have a WONDERFUL Holiday Season!"

Decorate your tree just like the Swamp Kids!

Contributed by Laurie Banfell & Sheryl Pedersen

FIRST...ASK AN ADULT TO HELP YOU.
(recommended for children 3 and above)

PINE CONE ORNAMENTS

Take some small **PINE CONES**; dab Elmer's Glue on the "scales," then place colored beads on the scales and sprinkle the whole cone with glitter. Take a red or green pipe cleaner and wrap it around the top of the cone on one end and fashion a loop around the other end.

Hang the cones on your tree just like the Swamp Kids!

POPCORN & CRANBERRY GARLANDS

Make a bag of microwave **BUTTER-FREE POPCORN** and place in a bowl. Careful, it could be hot! Open a bag of **FRESH CRANBERRIES** and place them in another bowl. With the help of an adult, string a long piece of thread through a needle and then push it through one or two pieces of popcorn separated with cranberries.......repeat the process. Once you have reached the end of the strand, tie it off and start another piece; once that piece is finished, tie them together. Continue until you have enough to wrap around your tree about 4 or 5 times. It will add a nice, homey touch to your tree.

Hint: Make sure and eat some of your popcorn while you're making your strands! Ask the rest of the family to join in!

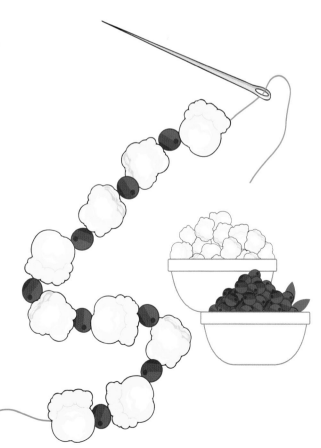

Join the Adventure!

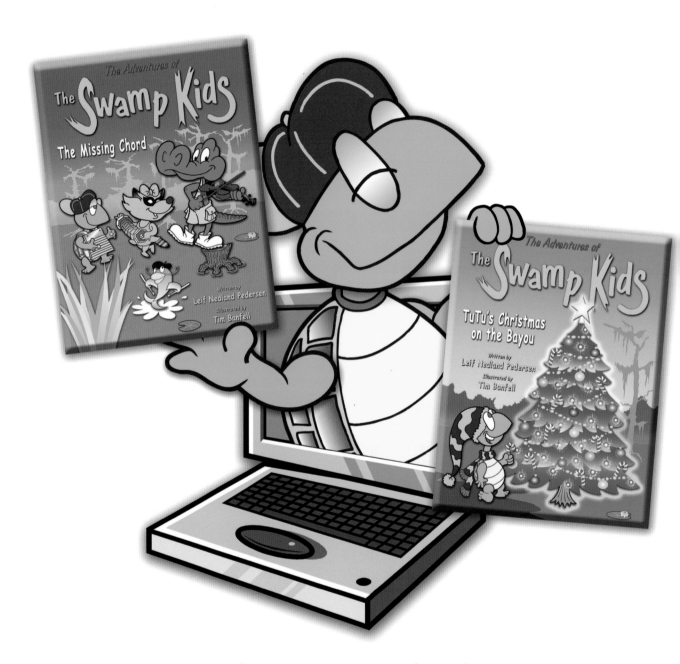

www.theswampkids.com